THE Truth About DRAGONS

by Tracy Sue Walker

illustrated by Richard Watson

SCHOLASTIC INC.

Special thanks to Hanif Sufizada for his invaluable help with this book.

ISBN 978-1-338-67094-3

10 9 8 7 6 5 4 3 2 1   21 22 23 24 25

Printed in the U.S.A.   40
First printing 2021

Book design by Jennifer Rinaldi

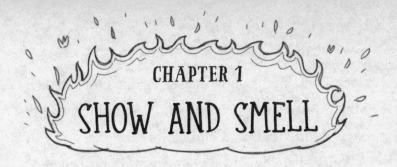

CHAPTER 1
SHOW AND SMELL

Here's a question for you. What's the difference between a dragon and a hot-air balloon?

The answer—nothing!

They're both huge. They both fly. And they're both full of hot air.

I'm Julian Fillmore. My friends Sarah Marco, Ava Chen, and I are sick and tired of magical creatures—Magicals—hogging the spotlight. That's why we started The Kids for Truth about Magical Creatures (KTMC). Ordinaries—non-magical creatures—are always pushed to the side, forgotten, and ignored.

We're here to do something about it.

KTMC will prove that Magicals aren't all that. And dragons? Nothing to get fired up about.

BLOOP, BLOOP, BLOOP. The plastic mermaid

clock is making bubble noises again. Our teacher, Mrs. Frisner, won it when she mailed in thirty empty bags of Puffy Pals marshmallows.

Puffy Pals is always having Magical-themed contests. Send in ten empty bags and win a Bigfoot wristwatch. Draw the best picture of a troll, win a year's supply of marshmallows. You get the picture.

The clock is the size of a tennis racquet and has curly blonde hair with seashell combs. Her tail is green with the Puffy Pals logo on her fin, and the motor making it swing back and forth sounds like a fly trapped in a jar. "It's eleven o'clock!" she says in a high-pitched squeak. "Have a FIN-tastic day!" BLOOP, BLOOP, BLOOP. Ava thinks the clock is the only thing more annoying than a real mermaid.

Mrs. Frisner brushes past my desk as she walks to the front of the room. Her overalls are pink and covered with pictures of garden gnomes wearing red and purple hats. She loves Magicals. That's why our classroom is covered in them. Unicorn decals, ogre photos, dragon posters—you name it, we've got it!

The overalls have a pocket on the front where she

keeps the markers for the white board. She takes one out and writes *Show and Tell* in big red letters.

"Class!" she says. Her voice sounds like sandpaper rubbing against gravel. "Put your worksheets away."

You never know what you're going to get with Show and Tell in Mrs. Frisner's class. So far, we've seen everything from Brandon Henderson's unicorn, Sugar, to Allison Winder's diorama of Mount Rushmore. She carved the whole thing out of her mom's old scented candles. For the next three days, our classroom smelled like a weird combination of apple pie and ocean breeze. Ever since then, Sarah's called it Show and Smell.

"Who wants to go first?" Mrs. Frisner asks.

Spencer Jacobson walks to the front of the room. She opens her hand to show us what she brought. It's a cotton ball.

"My uncle gave me this," she says. "It's a magical seed. You plant it on a full moon and water it every day, and in twenty-nine days, you'll grow a cloud."

Ava's hand shoots up. Mrs. Frisner takes a deep breath, "Yes, Miss Chen."

"That's impossible," Ava says. "We know from science that—"

Before Ava can finish her sentence, Mrs. Frisner cuts in. "Thank you, Spencer. NEXT!"

Madison Rainwater walks to the front with her kayak paddle.

"Every summer, my family goes on a camping trip," she says.

She's wearing her hiking boots. There are so many mud stains on them, you can't tell what color they were originally. That's what I like about Madison; she isn't interested in what things look like on the outside.

"The best part about camping is kayaking. And sometimes you get to meet new friends," she says and smiles at me.

Mrs. Frisner tries not to yawn, "Lovely, Miss Rainwater. NEXT!"

Najeeb Ahmadi stands and carries something that looks like a fish tank to the display table. There's a dark purple cloth draped over it, and when he lifts it, there's a terrarium underneath with a branch, a fake rock, and an orange plastic plant inside.

Mrs. Frisner leans forward and squints. "Tell us about . . . that, Mr. Ahmadi."

"I made the rock myself. It's papier-mâché, and my dad helped me build the motor, so it's heated." Najeeb's always making things—bots, rubber-band cars, a machine that blows bubbles.

"Very nice, Mr. Ahmadi," Mrs. Frisner says. "Does it do anything . . . else?"

Najeeb clears his throat, "I brought Tiger. My leopard gecko." Everybody leans forward, but there's nothing else to see. "He's nocturnal, so he's asleep inside his rock right now." There's silence, and he hunches his shoulders. "Did you know leopard geckos can regrow their tails if they lose them?" More silence. Najeeb shuffles his feet. "And they're great at hiding!"

"We can see that," Mrs. Frisner says. "Does anyone have any questions for Mr. Ahmadi?"

Brandon Henderson raises his hand, "Does he eat butterflies? I've heard geckos eat butterflies."

Before Najeeb can answer, a tiny voice comes out

of the rock. "Skinks eat butterflies. I'm a gecko."

Madison's hand goes up. "Does he breathe through his skin?"

The tiny voice yawns, "Salamanders. Not geckos."

"Can we see him change colors?" Ben Hinklemeyer asks.

"I am NOT a chameleon." The voice is louder this time, and Tiger's spotted head peeks out from his rock.

"He's beautiful!" Madison says.

Tiger has golden-yellow skin with black spots all over, and he glistens in the overhead lights. He comes out of his rock and creeps to the middle of his terrarium.

"I'm not a chameleon," he says again. "But I am a comedian!" He stands on his hind legs. "Good evening, ladies and germs. Why are Komodo dragons such good storytellers?"

He pauses. "Because they have tails!"

Everybody laughs. "Thank you, folks. I'm here all day!" Tiger bows and runs back inside his rock.

"Come back out!" someone shouts.

"Is he a Magical?" someone else asks.

"He's just an extraordinary Ordinary!" Najeeb says.

I look over at Ava and Sarah. We're all smiling. Finally, an Ordinary is getting the respect he deserves.

Mrs. Frisner sits down at her desk. "He's a laugh riot, Mr. Ahmadi. NEXT!"

Everybody watches Najeeb go back to his desk with Tiger, but I watch Lily Threadgill stand and carry her backpack to the front of the room. She pulls at the zipper.

"Good gremlins!" Mrs. Frisner shouts. All heads snap around. "Is . . . is that . . . ?"

Lily opens her backpack. Show and Smell will never be the same.

CHAPTER 2
EGG-STRORDINARY!

"Is that . . . ?" Mrs. Frisner tries again. She rubs her hands together and taps her feet like it's the last day of school.

Lily lifts an egg out of her backpack. It's the size of a golf ball, and she holds it up so everyone can see. It's bright turquoise and the shell is pearly and swirly. When it catches the light, it looks like someone dumped a whole bottle of glitter over it, and it's so bright Ava shields her eyes.

I blink a few times to make sure my eyes aren't playing tricks. The egg is growing. It's the size of a tennis ball now.

Mrs. Frisner clutches her favorite Magical mug. It's a green dragon with dark, baggy circles under her eyes. She's wearing curlers, and her tail forms the handle. The back of the mug says, "My feet are draggin' without coffee."

I look from Mrs. Frisner to the mug to the egg. A

light bulb goes on in my brain. Mrs. Frisner doesn't have to say it. I know what Lily Threadgill brought to Show and Smell.

"Is that a dragon egg?" Mrs. Frisner finally spits out.

Lily nods, and the whole classroom breaks out in cheers. I look over at Ava and Sarah, but the three of us aren't celebrating.

I glance back at Najeeb. Tiger stands on his hind legs with his front paws and nose pressed to the glass of his terrarium. As soon as he hears what Lily brought, he slides down the glass, hangs his head, and shuffles back inside his rock. So much for Ordinaries getting their turn in the spotlight.

"Where'd you get it?" Ben Hinkelmeyer asks.

"My mom," Lily answers.

"Where'd she get it?" Ben says.

"She's egg-sitting for someone at work," Lily says. "I'm taking care of it today. Keeping it warm. It should hatch in a week or two."

Lily's mom, Dr. Threadgill, works at the art museum. She's in the Medieval Art and Architecture wing. Last year she came to our class and talked about castles, and then each of us had to build a model of one at home using sugar cubes. Mine fell apart when my mom hit a pothole on our ride to school. We're still finding sugar cubes under the back seat of our minivan.

Mrs. Frisner moves toward the egg, never taking her eyes off it.

"What kind of dragon egg is it?" Sarah asks.

"I don't know," Lily says. "Dr. Ember's helping mom with a new exhibit. She flew in from Scotland."

Mrs. Frisner runs to the world map at the back of the classroom. She's a blur of gray hair and garden gnomes.

"Is she a Cornish Crested?" Mrs. Frisner asks,

pointing to the southwestern tip of England. The map has at least 100 tiny flags, each with a different Magical written on it, pinned to their native land. There are dragon flags on all seven continents.

"I don't know," Lily answers.

Mrs. Frisner points to another flag. "Is she a Londinium Short Wing?"

"I'm not sure," Lily says.

"A Yorkshire Club Tail?"

"Uh . . . maybe . . . ," Lily says.

"Norman Fireless?"

Lily shrugs.

I glance at Tiger's terrarium. Najeeb presses his forehead to the glass and taps gently, but Tiger doesn't come back out. I catch Ava's eye, then Sarah's. I get out my worksheet, write "Emergency Meeting?" on the back, and hold it up so they can see. They both nod in agreement as the bell rings for lunch.

Lily carefully sets the egg back inside her backpack. It's the size of a softball now.

Najeeb lugs Tiger's terrarium to the back of the room by his cubby.

"We have to do something to cheer Tiger up," Sarah says. "Anybody know a joke?"

"Here's one," Ava says. "How many Ordinaries does it take to change a light bulb?"

Sarah shakes her head.

"It doesn't matter," Ava answers. "Nobody cares anyway."

"But KTMC cares," I say. "Let's make a pact. Tiger will get his day in the spotlight."

Our blog, Creature Feature, is the perfect place to make that happen. Sarah keeps notes of our investigations, Ava takes photos, and I write the blog. We expose Magicals for the doughnuts they are—all sprinkles and icing on the outside, nothing in the middle.

I stick out my arm and lay my hand flat. Ava does the same thing, laying her hand on top of mine. Sarah follows, laying her hand on Ava's.

"All for one," I say.

Ava and Sarah join in, "And all for Ordinaries!"

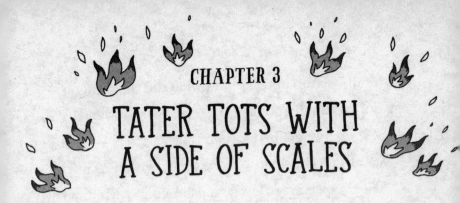

CHAPTER 3

TATER TOTS WITH A SIDE OF SCALES

As I walk through the cafeteria door, I take a deep breath before I'm hit full force with nuclear-strength green-bean smell.

We go through the lunch line, and Mrs. Earp piles our trays high with casserole. It's made with last Tuesday's fish sticks and tater tots.

Everybody at our class table is trying to sit next to Lily Threadgill, even though she left the egg in our classroom. They've moved their chairs to form a semicircle around her. Najeeb and Madison Rainwater are the only two people at the other end until we sit down.

Ava breaks the ice; she's good at that. "Look, Najeeb, it's an egg. Big deal. I can think of lots of eggs more exciting than a dragon egg. Scrambled eggs, for example."

"Yeah," Sarah agrees, "and what did that dragon egg do? Nothing! You have a leopard gecko who tells jokes. It doesn't get better than that."

Najeeb cracks a smile. "Tiger's pretty great, isn't he?"

"Tiger's spots are so lovely, and he's funny," Madison adds. "Beauty and brains!"

"And what do we really know about dragons, anyway?" I say. "It's all rumors. They hide away in their caves and dens. It's a mystery."

"Like this casserole," Sarah adds.

"They hoard treasure," Ava says. "That's a scientific fact."

"Says who?" Sarah asks.

"The Journal of Magical Creatures. They published a study last summer. You want to see the world's largest emerald? Too bad. It's in a dragon's private collection." Ava goes on, "How about the purest chunk of gold? Same thing. Finest silk ever spun? Guess who's hoarding that?"

"Not a leopard gecko, that's for sure," Najeeb says.

"Exactly." Ava goes on, "They're snobby, too. They look down their overheated noses at everybody—even other Magicals."

"That explains DINO," I say.

"What's that?" Madison asks.

"Dragon International Networking Organization. From what I hear, if you're not hoarding a big enough treasure, you don't get in," I say. "If the rumors are true, dragons are total wet blankets, too. You'll never see a dragon do stand-up, like Tiger. No senses of humor."

"Why did the dragon cross the road?" Ava asks.

Najeeb scrunches his eyebrows. "Why?"

"No one will ever know," Ava answers, popping a tater tot into her mouth. "They'd never let you finish the joke."

"My mom had to get an expert opinion for her show once," Sarah says. Her mom produces Afternoon Art Talk for our public radio station. "The expert was a dragon. The only way she could reach him was by writing a letter. On paper. With a pen. Can you believe that? They're so behind the times."

"And they're terrible cooks," I add. "My dad gets Delectable Dishes every month. The recipes from Magicals are usually pretty good, except dragons.

They burn everything to a crisp. Every recipe requires a blow torch. But there's one way we can figure out the truth once and for all."

"Dragons should be our next investigation," Sarah says.

"Our last class is in the media center today," Ava says. "We can start our research."

"Hey, Najeeb," I say, "can we interview Tiger for Creature Feature? Would he tell us about being an Ordinary trying to compete with that dragon egg?"

Najeeb nods. "Sure—I'll bring him to school tomorrow."

"I hope it makes him feel better," Sarah says. "It's not easy being upstaged by a dragon."

Najeeb reaches down with his fork and spears the last tot in his casserole. "Tiger knows a lot about dragons," he says as the bell rings. "Especially after what happened to his tail."

Ava, Sarah, and I look at each other. What's the tale behind Tiger's tail?

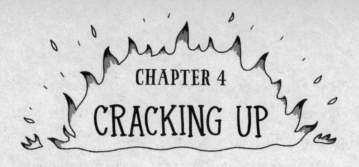

CHAPTER 4
CRACKING UP

"DID YOU KNOW NEBRASKA HAS THIS THING CALLED Carhenge?" Ava asks out loud to no one in particular. "It's thirty-nine old cars arranged like Stonehenge. Incredible!" She looks at me out of the corner of her eye and says under her breath, "Is she gone?"

I nod, watching Mrs. Hart, our media specialist, walk away. We're supposed to be finding information on the fifty states for social studies, but Carhenge can wait, dragons can't.

"I found something!" Sarah whispers to me and Ava, and she tilts her computer screen so we can see the article. It's from our local newspaper. "World Renowned Expert Shares Collection at Museum of Art and Architecture," it reads.

Sarah opens her notebook to jot a few things down, and that's when I notice the sketch. It's the dragon egg, with its pearly swirly shell, plus she's drawn little starbursts and fancy hearts all over the page.

"You a fan?" I ask her.

"Of course not," she says. "It's art . . . and research." She shuts the notebook so fast I can't see if there are any more sketches, but I get the feeling Sarah might be as mesmerized by that egg as the rest of our class.

"'Doctor Ernestine Ember, the world's leading expert on magical tapestries, is working with Doctor Emily Threadgill of the Museum of Art and Architecture, to showcase four pieces from her private collection,'" Sarah reads.

"From her private hoard," Ava says.

Sarah goes on, "'The magical tapestries date back one thousand years and are priceless, having been woven entirely from unicorn hair.'" She stops reading and looks at me and Ava. "I know these tapestries! My mom gave me a book about them when I got interested in fiber arts!"

"What kind of arts?" I ask.

"You know, things made from yarn and string. Weavings, tapestries," Sarah says. "I'll get to see them in person. I can't believe it. The color of the unicorn hair changes depending on who's looking at the tapestry. It's different for every person. They're incredible!"

"Don't get too excited. They're hoarded by a dragon, remember?" I say.

Mrs. Hart rounds the corner again. I give Ava a look, and she jumps right in. "And that's why New Mexico has more cows than people! Who knew?"

"I'm glad you're finding lots of wonderful information," Mrs. Hart says and smiles at the three of us.

Once she's gone, Ava turns her computer screen toward me and Sarah. "Can't Sleep? Call a Dragon," it says, and Ava reads from the screen. "'The history of socks, envelopes, and pencil erasers. To the average person, these topics might seem boring, but to a dragon, they're fascinating.'"

"Evidently, dragons are nerdy know-it-alls," Ava adds.

"That sounds familiar," I say.

She sighs. "The article mentions that it's common for a dragon to talk about their favorite topic for five or six hours without stopping."

"Five hours on the history of pencil erasers. That's worse than Frisner's social studies class," I say.

"It also says talking to a dragon is the number-one best cure if you can't sleep," Ava says.

"But the trick is finding a dragon. They're really rare," I say and turn my computer screen so the others can see the article I found from Treasure Hunter Quarterly. "It says dragons are the greediest of all Magicals. They hoard treasure, and they never share. Gold. Emeralds. Diamonds. Art. But baby dragons are worth more than any of it."

"What? Why?" Sarah asks.

"It says a baby dragon will lead anybody or anything to its mother's treasure hoard. No questions asked," I say and glance across the media center at Lily Threadgill. Her backpack is on the floor next to her. It's bulging and looks like it's about to burst open. The egg must be the size of a basketball now.

Mrs. Hart rounds the corner again. "And that's why you'll get fined if you throw pickle juice off a streetcar in Rhode Island," Ava says.

"I can't wait to read these reports," Mrs. Hart says with a smile. "So many interesting facts you're finding."

When the bell rings, everybody makes a mad dash. Sarah and I follow Ava to her locker, and Najeeb walks past, lugging the terrarium. Tiger's still hiding inside his heated rock.

"We need a plan for the interview," I say.

"Najeeb said Tiger knows a lot about dragons. We should try to find out what that's about," Sarah says as the school door slams behind him. We're the only ones left except Lily Threadgill at the other end of the hall.

"What's she doing?" Ava asks.

"Beats me. I think she's fighting with her backpack," I say. "Looks like the backpack's winning."

Lily's groans echo all the way down the hall.

"She needs help. C'mon!" Sarah says and takes off running.

The zipper on Lily's backpack busts open. The dragon egg that was only the size of a golf ball during

Show and Smell is as huge as a watermelon now. It rolls out of the busted backpack and lays in the middle of the hall, rocking back and forth. There's tapping coming from inside the egg.

"Can we help?" Sarah asks.

Lily nods. "I have to get it back inside."

"I don't think that's going to happen," I say. Her backpack looks like an alligator used it for a chew toy.

"Hey! What's happening?" Ava asks, pointing at the egg.

It's still rocking, but now it's also changing colors like Christmas tree lights. It fades from red to purple, then blue to green. Over and over. The tapping gets louder.

"What are we going to do?" Lily asks.

"*We?*" Ava says. "*You* brought the dragon egg to Show and Smell!"

"C'mon, she needs our help," Sarah says, and while they try to fix Lily's backpack, I watch the egg.

"Uh . . . guys . . . ," I say.

"I think if we tie the straps like this, it could work," Ava says.

"Hey . . . guys . . . ," I try again.

"No, it needs to go like this," Sarah says, turning the bag and fiddling with the broken zipper.

"I think you should see this . . . ," I say, a little louder.

"What if we turn it inside out?" Lily asks, taking what's left of her backpack from Sarah and Ava.

"Guys!" I point at the egg, which is the now size of a beach ball.

"That wouldn't fit in King Kong's backpack," Ava says.

It's perfectly still now. And silent.

The four of us bend over to pick it up and . . . CRACK!

CHAPTER 5
OH BABY!

THE TAPPING STARTS AGAIN AND GETS LOUDER AND louder, and the crack on the egg's shell gets bigger. No one moves.

A small dragon nose with pink-rimmed nostrils breaks through the top of the egg.

"What do we do now?" Lily asks.

"We should help," Sarah says, bending over the egg and pushing pieces of shell away. Little puffs of smoke rise from its pink nostrils until its nose twitches, "Ah . . . ah . . . ah . . . CHOOOOOO!" The rest of the eggshell shatters and a bright turquoise baby dragon with purple claws sits in the middle of the hall. It hiccups and another puff of smoke rises.

"So, the article was right," Ava whispers. "A baby dragon is the same color as its egg."

The baby looks up at us with emerald eyes, and its pupils are long black slits—like Tiger's.

"Does it have a name?" Sarah asks.

Lily shakes her head. "I don't think so. Mom didn't mention it."

"I think there's a way we can find out," I say. "One of those articles said all baby dragons are born with their names on their bellies. It takes a few days for their scales to harden, and then the name disappears."

"Should we check?" Lily asks.

"There's that we again," Ava says.

I turn to Sarah. "It trusts you. You want to try?" By now the baby dragon has locked its big green eyes on Sarah and is cooing softly.

Sarah leans over again and reaches out to stroke the baby's nose. "You're okay. I won't hurt you. Hey . . . I'm stuck!" Her hand isn't moving.

"That's great!" Ava says, but Sarah doesn't look excited. "I read about this!" Ava goes on. "You know how pangolins have sticky spit so ants and bugs don't fall off their tongues when they're trying to catch dinner?"

"Of course, I know that!" I throw my hands in the air. "Who doesn't spend most of their free time reading about pangolins?"

Ava rolls her eyes at me. "It's the same thing with dragons, only they have the ability to make their scales sticky. It helps them carry things. Treasure, books, baby dragons . . . ," she says. "It takes them a while to learn how to turn it on and off, though."

"Great, now you tell me," Sarah says, prying her hand off the baby's nose. Little puffs of smoke rise from its nostrils again, and it rolls over on its back with its belly in the air.

Sure enough, there's writing. The letters are faint. Ghost letters. And the writing looks old like it does on the Declaration of Independence.

"How do you say that?" Sarah asks.

"Call-dare-ah," Ava says. "Like the hollow top of a volcano after it erupts."

"Caldera," Sarah repeats. "That's pretty. You think it's a girl?"

"From what my mom told me, I'm pretty sure it

is," Lily says, and she sits on the floor next to Sarah. The baby waves her little feet in the air, then her nose twitches again. "Ah . . . ah . . . ah . . . CHOOOOO!" This time tiny sparks shoot from her mouth and two small wings unfurl. One of the sparks lands on what's left of Lily's backpack.

"Watch out!" Ava says, stomping on it. "She'll set off the sprinklers."

Before any of us can stop her, Caldera rolls back over. She flaps her wings harder and harder until she lifts off the ground. She's two feet in the air when she belly-flops. She tries again. Another belly flop. She tries a third time. Same thing. Her forehead wrinkles and more puffs of smoke spill from her nostrils.

She flaps her wings, and I think she's going to try to fly again, but she takes off running down the hall.

"Hey!" Lily calls, running after her, and we all follow. Her tiny purple claws click-clack all the way down the hall. The door to Ava's locker is still open, and she's heading straight for it, wings flapping.

"Airborne!" I yell. Caldera's wings carry her higher and higher. Two feet. Three feet. Four.

There's a round gold magnet on the door of Ava's locker, and it's holding a photo of scientist Marie Curie. Caldera stuffs the whole thing in her mouth.

"That doesn't belong to you!" Ava shouts. She wrestles the photo away, and it's still in one piece. Caldera tries to grab another magnet. This one's holding a photo of a large, blurry figure walking through the woods. "Don't even think about it!" Ava says, grabbing it before it's too late.

"She can't help it," Lily says. "Dragons love shiny things."

We all stop when we hear Mrs. Frisner's voice outside the door to the building. She's yelling at some kid about chewing gum at school.

"We need to do something—fast!" I say.

"I can't believe I'm helping a dragon," Ava says, getting her own backpack out of her locker. Ava carries a lot of books, so it's extra big and strong. "Hurry!" She holds it open while Sarah, Lily, and I do our best to get Caldera tucked inside.

"Thank goodness she's not sticky right now," Sarah says.

We leave the backpack unzipped just enough so she can get fresh air.

The door opens, then slams shut behind Mrs. Frisner. She crosses her arms and barks, "Why are you still here?"

"I thought I lost my camera. They were helping me look for it," Ava says, patting her bulging backpack. "Found it!"

"Then hit the road!" Mrs. Frisner says. "You four are the only things standing between me and a bag of marshmallows."

The four of us shuffle out of the building as fast as we can, and when the door slams shut, we all let out a huge sigh.

"That was close," Sarah says.

"Speaking of close, we'll walk home with you," I say to Lily. "You might need help with Caldera."

"My backpack's going to need help by the time Baby Volcano is done with it," Ava grumbles.

We take turns carrying it. A baby dragon isn't exactly light.

"I know what you were reading about in the

media center," Lily says while we walk.

"New Mexico?" Ava asks, looking at me out of the corner of her eye.

Lily laughs. "Nice try. I'm not Mrs. Hart. I saw your computer screen when I walked past to go to the restroom."

No one says anything.

"There's a lot of bad information out there that says all dragons are terrible. And selfish. And snobby," Lily says. "But most of it isn't true."

"How do you know?" Ava raises her eyebrow.

"I've gotten to know Dr. Ember a little bit," Lily says. "She's not boring, that's for sure. And she doesn't hoard treasure . . . well, maybe she hoards a little bit, but who am I to judge? I have over one hundred mermaid action figures at home."

"Ava loves mermaids," I say, and she gives me a dirty look.

While we walk, Lily talks about her mom and the museum. Even though we've been in the same class since kindergarten, I don't know Lily all that well, but here are three things I do know about her:

1) She's super smart. Not Ava smart, but close.

2) She travels a lot with her mom and wears interesting clothes from other countries. Today, she's wearing a vest from Peru made with lots of different colored thread.

3) She loves words, like me. She's always writing.

I hand her the backpack when we reach her house.

"Thank you," she says to all of us, "I don't know what I would've done without your help."

"You'd be Frisner's prisoner," I say. "Puffy Pals has a new contest—send in a selfie with a Magical, win a ten-foot inflatable dragon. She'd take five hundred selfies with Caldera to get the perfect shot of them roasting marshmallows with dragon breath. You'd be there until midnight."

Lily laughs and unzips the backpack a little more so she can give it back.

"It's okay," Ava says. "Bring it back tomorrow. You don't want her to run off before you get inside."

Without warning, Lily throws her arms around Ava.

"Oh! Okay," Ava says, giving Lily a couple of awkward pats on the back. "I'm not really a . . .

hugger . . ."

Lily lets go and carefully picks up the squirming backpack.

"Good luck!" I holler as she walks toward her house. Another puff of smoke rises from the backpack.

"That was really nice of you," Sarah says, turning to Ava and spreading her arms wide. "You deserve another hug!"

"You do and you die," Ava crosses her arms.

Sarah laughs. "Caldera was pretty cute. I've never seen a baby dragon before."

"But she'll turn into a grown one," I say. "And there's nothing cute about that. Just ask Tiger."

"Yeah, what's that all about?" Sarah asks.

"We'll find out tomorrow," I answer. Greedy, snooty, ferocious dragons are about to go up in smoke!

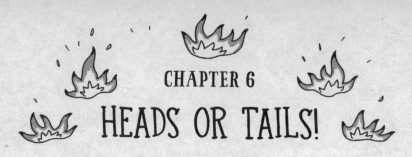

CHAPTER 6
HEADS OR TAILS!

"Is he coming?" Ava's tapping her foot. "We're busy people. We all have lives."

"Here he comes." I point as Najeeb walks out of the school building.

"Remember, we have to be fair," Sarah says. "There are two sides to every story, even if the other side is from a dragon."

When Najeeb reaches the playground benches where we hold our KTMC meetings, he sets a black plastic carrier the size of a shoebox next to me. I point at it, "Your box is humming."

"Oh yeah," Najeeb says. "I built another motor, so it stays warm for Tiger."

"Is he ready?" I ask. Along with our blog, we're starting a Creature Feature podcast, and Sarah's mom is going to show us how to put it together. She let us borrow a voice recorder for Tiger's interview. I set it between me and the carrier.

"Ready as he'll ever be," Najeeb says. He opens a small hatch on the roof of the carrier and reaches in. "C'mon buddy," he says.

There's no question Tiger's ready. As soon as Najeeb sets him next to the recorder, he stands on his hind legs and holds a piece of pine straw like it's a microphone. Ava has her camera ready and starts snapping photos.

"What a great lookin' audience!" he says. "Here's one I heard just the other day. Knock knock?"

"Who's there?" we all say.

"Cash," Tiger says.

"Cash who?" we ask.

"No, thanks," Tiger says. "I'll have a peanut instead!" Sarah giggles.

"Get it? Cashew! Like the nut? While we're on the subject of nuts, are you ready to interview this one?" Tiger asks, pointing to himself.

I turn the recorder on and ask the first question. "So, Tiger, can you tell us a little about leopard geckos? Where are you from?"

"Easy-peasy," Tiger says. "You'll find us in

Afghanistan, parts of India . . . Deserts and grasslands are right up our alley. Personally, I spent a lot of time in the mountains, but that's just me. I went there to think about things, practice my jokes . . ."

Sarah nods. "So, what do you like to eat?"

"I haven't met a cricket or mealworm I didn't like," Tiger says. "But cockroaches, not so much. They leave a bad aftertaste."

Ava looks like *she* bit into a cockroach. "I didn't need to know that," she says under her breath.

"And how did you meet Najeeb," I ask.

"Best day of my life. I was his uncle's friend first, right?" Tiger says.

Najeeb nods and Tiger continues.

"Najeeb's uncle goes all over the world. He's a rock expert, especially heavy metals," Tiger says.

"A rock music expert!" Sarah's eyes widen.

Tiger chuckles and shakes his head. "Rock expert—mountains, boulders, layers of earth."

"A geologist," Ava says.

Tiger nods and flicks his long tongue out at something buzzing in the air. He swallows. "House fly. Delicious!"

"I didn't need to know that, either," Ava mutters.

"I'm from Afghanistan, and so is Najeeb's uncle. He was on a dig in the mountains, and I helped him find iron ore. From that day on, we were a team. Traveled all over the world. Africa, South America, Australia—seen 'em all! But when I met Najeeb, I knew I was home."

"Tiger told my uncle he was retiring from the field. He decided to stay with my family instead," Najeeb says.

"How did your uncle feel about that?" Sarah asks.

"He was sad to lose Tiger, but happy we were together. Afghanistan is very far away. I've only been to visit once when I was a baby, so I don't get to see my grandparents, and uncles and aunts very often." Najeeb is quiet for a minute, and Tiger pats his knee.

"My uncle told me," Najeeb says, "'When you are missing us and we feel very far away, hold Tiger close to your heart and know your family is there, too. Just a heartbeat away.'"

"It's getting a little heavy here, buddy," Tiger says, still patting Najeeb's knee. "Time to lighten the mood. What's a dragon's favorite day of the week?"

We all shrug.

"It's Chewsday!" Tiger's trying not to laugh at his own joke. "Get it?" he looks up at Najeeb. "Chewsday?" Najeeb smiles. "There it is!" Tiger says. "I knew I could make it come back."

"Since you mentioned dragons," I say to Tiger. "What can you tell us?"

He swallows hard and thumps his tail. "Oh, I can tell you about dragons, all right."

We all lean forward to get a better look. Up close, the coloring on Tiger's tail looks a little different than the rest of his body.

"What happened?" Sarah asks.

"I was with Najeeb's uncle. We were climbing a mountain on our way to a dig, studying rubies. We made it halfway up, at least five hundred feet, when the mountain started moving. Everything shook. We thought it was an earthquake." Tiger closes his eyes and takes a deep breath.

"You okay, buddy?" Najeeb asks.

Tiger nods and goes on, "Then we realized, we weren't standing on the mountain anymore, we were standing on the head of a Craggy-Scaled dragon. It moved its enormous tail first, trying to swat us off. Boulders crashed around us."

"Craggy-Scaled?" I ask.

"Their scales blend in with rock. Perfect for hiding," Najeeb says. "You can't tell where the mountain ends and the dragon begins. America has them, too, in the Rocky Mountains."

"Why haven't we heard about that?" I ask Ava

and Sarah.

"They're extremely rare," Najeeb says. "It's next to impossible to catch a glimpse of one, that's why."

"But you did?" Sarah asks Tiger.

"There were flames burning inside its red eyes," Tiger says, taking another deep breath. "It was at least forty feet tall."

"What did it want?" Ava asks.

"Dragons are greedy Magicals," Tiger says. "It didn't want us finding its rubies. And who's going to stand up to a moving mountain that can roast you like a marshmallow? Not this gecko, that's for sure!"

"What did it do next?" I ask.

"It looked down its snout at us and snorted puffs of smoke." Tiger shudders. "That's when Najeeb's uncle grabbed me, and we got off that mountain as fast as we could."

"So . . . it didn't hurt you?" Ava asks.

Tiger shakes his head, "No, but I was so scared. I couldn't help it . . . I . . . I . . ." Tiger buries his head in his paws. "I dropped my tail."

"Dropped your tail?" I ask. "Like . . . literally,

your tail fell off?"

Sarah gasps.

"Geckos do that," Tiger says, "when we're really scared. But it's okay; they grow back." He turns around and wiggles his tail to show us.

We're all quiet—even Ava—until Tiger claps his paws together. "Enough with the long faces! Hey, what does a gecko do when he loses his tail?" He pauses. "He goes to the retail store! Get it? ReTAIL store. Ha!" That gets us all smiling again.

"So being upstaged by that dragon egg really hurt," Sarah says.

"More than you know," Tiger says with a nod.

I turn the recorder off. "I think that's a great place to end to the interview," I say. "Thanks, Tiger. I think we have a much better idea of what dragons are really like."

"Worse than we thought," Ava says.

Even Sarah nods. "I'm glad you found each other," she says to Najeeb and Tiger.

"Me too." Najeeb picks Tiger up and opens the hatch on the carrier. "Ready to go home, buddy?"

"Ready!" Tiger says. "Thanks, folks! You've been a great audience."

We watch Najeeb and Tiger walk across the parking lot to his mom's car.

Ava crosses her arms. "Dragons are worse than I thought."

"But we're not hearing that dragon's side of the story," Sarah says, brushing pine straw off the bench. "It was minding its own business on that mountain."

"Yeah, but what kind of creature would do that—scare someone so badly their tail falls off?" Ava asks. "Bunnies don't do that sort of thing."

Sarah nods, "True. And that had to be really scary for Tiger."

"Either way, we need to interview a dragon." I stand and sling my backpack over my shoulder, and that's when I think of Lily. "And I know where we can find one!"

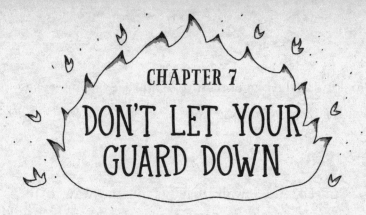

CHAPTER 7
DON'T LET YOUR GUARD DOWN

AVA STICKS HER TONGUE OUT AT THE CLOCK WHEN it tells the time.

BLOOP, BLOOP, BLOOP. "It's eight o'clock!" the mermaid says with a giggle. "Have a FIN-tastic day!" BLOOP, BLOOP, BLOOP.

"Class," Mrs. Frisner croaks before we get out our science books. "Dr. Threadgill invited us to see her new exhibit this morning before it opens to the public."

Sarah flashes a thumbs-up at me, but Ava raises her hand.

Mrs. Frisner takes a deep breath like she's sipping air through a straw. "Yes, Miss Chen."

"Will we have science when we get back?"

"That's doubtful," Mrs. Frisner says.

Ava groans. She only has eyes for science, but I'm

looking at the bigger picture. And I see one interview with a dragon coming up!

Najeeb and I walk together on the way to the museum complex. He points to the baseball cap he's wearing and whispers, "I have a stowaway."

"Tiger?" I ask, and he nods.

Najeeb lifts his baseball cap just enough to show me the smiling gecko underneath.

"My terrarium's so boring when Najeeb's not home," Tiger whispers.

The museum complex is one of my favorite places. All the museums are connected by underground tunnels. The Museum of Art and Architecture is connected to the Natural History Museum, which is connected to the Museum of Space and Exploration, which is connected to the aquarium.

Mrs. Frisner leads us through galleries of paintings and sculptures until we reach the Hall of Armor.

"This place is spooky," Ava says, looking around.

"Really spooky," Tiger says, peeking out from

Najeeb's cap.

All the suits are lined up like they're ready for battle and could come to life at any minute. Dr. Threadgill is standing in a big archway at the end of the hall, waving at us. She has red frizzy hair that's piled in a bun with a pencil sticking out, and her chunky necklace looks like a bunch of tree bark someone strung together.

"Class," Dr. Threadgill says as we follow her into her tapestry exhibit. "Please say hello to our exhibit guard Mr. Hobb. He takes good care of these treasures and makes sure nobody steals them."

Mr. Hobb smiles, but his lip curls and it's more like a sneer.

"Okay, he's creepy, too," Ava whispers as we walk past, and I agree with her.

Dr. Threadgill leads us to a wall with a large white curtain draped across so we can't see what's behind it.

"You'll meet my partner, Dr. Ember, a little later. She was attending a family event in Europe yesterday and just flew back in from Scotland this morning," she says. "Her cousin lives in a lake there and just celebrated her 1,500th birthday."

"Her cousin must be Nessie!" Sarah whispers.

"So, the Loch Ness Monster *does exist*?" Najeeb asks.

"Yup," Ava says. "And it seems *everybody* knows her. Except us."

"Dr. Ember is catching up on emails," Dr. Threadgill goes on. "In the meantime, Lily and I are baby dragon-sitting. After you see the exhibit, I'll introduce you to Caldera." Our class bursts into applause with Mrs. Frisner clapping the loudest.

While Dr. Threadgill is explaining what we're about to see, I whisper to Lily, "Interviewing a dragon is the only way we can do a full investigation. Can we interview Dr. Ember while we're here?" I know it's a long shot, but I've got to try.

Lily bites her lip. I think that means "no."

"Without further ado," Dr. Threadgill says, pulling a gold rope with a tassel at the end. "I present the world-famous Magical tapestries from the collection of Dr. Ernestine Ember." The curtain falls, and everybody gasps.

"It's so much better than the photographs in my book," Sarah says. "The unicorns are neon pink!"

"No, they're not," Ava disagrees. "They're blue."

"My unicorns are yellow with black spots," Tiger says. "Like me."

"I don't know what you three are looking at," I say. "The unicorns are purple."

"It's different for everybody, remember," Sarah says. "They're woven with unicorn hair. That's what makes them magical."

While kids push and shove to get a better look, Lily talks with her mom. Finally, she comes back. "My mom said we can ask Dr. Ember, but we can't be pests. Follow me," she whispers.

We sneak away while the rest of our class argues about the unicorns. Lily leads us through a small door at the back of the exhibit and into storage. The ceilings are at least thirty feet high, and it looks like a warehouse. Our shoes squeak on the cement floor, and we walk past shelves stacked high with crates until we come around a corner.

We freeze.

"Leaping lizards!" Tiger gasps, peeking out from under Najeeb's cap. And he's not kidding.

CHAPTER 8
RUMOR HAS IT!

I'VE SEEN LOTS OF MAGICALS, BUT NOTHING LIKE this. My knees shake, and I understand why Tiger dropped his tail when he saw that Craggy-Scaled dragon. Dr. Ember's purple scales are so smooth they shine, and her lime-green claws are like daggers. She's sitting at a banquet table that looks like it belongs in a castle.

"What else are you going to use for a desk if you're a dragon?" Ava whispers.

An enormous pair of bifocals sit perched on the end of Dr. Ember's nose, and she's sipping something out of an equally huge teacup.

Lily shouts, "Dr. Ember!"

"I guess if you're twenty feet tall, people have to shout so you can hear them," I whisper back to Ava.

"I brought some friends to meet you. They write a blog about Magicals. Can they interview you, please?"

Dr. Ember sets the giant teacup back on its saucer, turns her head, and stares down at us with golden-yellow eyes. I hold my breath waiting for a roar or fire to shoot out of her mouth. She yawns.

"Forgive me, loves. Long flight. My wings are killing me. Tea?" She holds up a huge teapot, and a tiny puff of smoke rises from her nose.

We look at one another, and we're not sure what to say. Tiger stays under Najeeb's hat.

"And of course, you may interview me," Dr. Ember says. "Ask me anything you like, and I'll tell you. Except my bank account number, of course." She taps a small plaque with the tip of her claw that says "A penny saved is a penny earned."

I clear my throat and shout extra loud so she can hear me, "Dr. Ember!"

"Oh good heavens, dear. Inside voice, please," she says.

"Dr. Ember," I say, quieter this time. "Humans, Ordinaries, and even other Magicals all think dragons are greedy. They say you hoard treasure. What do you have to say about that?"

Dr. Ember sighs and another puff of smoke rises toward the ceiling. "Rumors, dear. Unfortunately, there aren't enough of us to go around proving them wrong. We're busy with other things. So, the rumors grow, no matter how untrue."

"Are you saying dragons don't hoard treasure?" Ava says.

"Well now," Dr. Ember starts. "*Hoard* is a very harsh word. Protect is more like it. We dragons collect precious things so we can keep them safe. These fragile items need our help. Not all Magicals are as thoughtful, dear. Some want them only for themselves."

"We read a lot of articles that said dragons are snooty and boring," I say.

Dr. Ember adds a sugar cube to her tea and stirs with her claw. "Many of us are quite shy, dear." Her voice is soft and calm. "Most of us prefer to be in our books, reading about what we love. Making small talk doesn't come easily. 'How's the weather?' and what not. One can easily mistake shy for snooty if you don't know someone well."

"Then how do you explain DINO?" I ask.

"I'm a proud member, dear!" Dr. Ember says. "Our motto is 'We Know Everything.'"

"I want to join!" Ava blurts. Dr. Ember blows a smoke ring out her left nostril and chuckles.

"That's nice, dear," Dr. Ember takes a sip of tea, "but DINO is only for serious scholars."

Ava crosses her arms. "I'll prove I'm serious. Ask me anything about science."

Dr. Ember blows another smoke ring, and this one goes over Ava like a hula hoop.

"Go on, ask," Ava says. "I'm ready!"

"I'm sure you are, dear," Dr. Ember smirks. "Perhaps we'll consider membership when you've been studying science over five hundred years. That's the age of our youngest member."

"Never mind," Ava mumbles.

Dr. Ember cranes her neck to see Sarah's notebook. She's been sketching the whole time we've been back here.

"An artist!" Dr. Ember says.

Sarah looks up, and Dr. Ember gives her a big, sharp-toothy smile. "Let me see. Hold it up, please," she says, and Sarah lifts her notebook as high as she can.

Dr. Ember takes it from her and adjusts her glasses. "You're quite gifted. That's an amazing likeness. May I?" She pages through Sarah's sketchbook. "This one is my favorite!"

While she gazes at Sarah's sketch of Caldera coming out of her shell, Ava snaps photos for Creature Feature.

"I love your tapestries," Sarah says. "My mom gave

me a small loom for weaving. I'm not very good yet."

"Practice. That's all it takes," Dr. Ember says. "With your talent, you'll get it in no time." She turns the page, and it's a sketch of Tiger. "Who is this wee one?"

"He's my friend, ma'am," Najeeb says. Tiger lifts the baseball cap and peeks out from underneath.

"Well, I've never seen such a beautiful leopard gecko," Dr. Ember says, pouring another cup of tea. "Truly an exquisite specimen. Like a tiny dragon."

"I am NOT a dragon!" Tiger says, dropping the cap so he's out of sight again.

"Oh dear," Dr. Ember says with a frown. "I said the wrong thing."

"It's just that . . . ," Najeeb starts. "He, uh . . . it's difficult for him to . . . uh . . ."

Dr. Ember folds her paws in her lap, and Ava jumps in, "You know that whole 'dragons are greedy and snooty' business? Tiger knows all about that. A dragon scared him so badly he dropped his tail!"

"Oh, my dear," Dr. Ember says. Her voice is still low and warm. "I am sorry." She leans down and tries to lift the cap off Najeeb's head with the tips of her lime-green claws, but Tiger pulls it back down. "You know," she goes on, "most dragons are quite kind, but some can be very thoughtless, like the one who did that to you. And like many people, even the best of us can have bad days every now and then."

"That's no excuse!" Ava says.

Lily looks uncomfortable. She's biting her bottom lip again. "Dr. Ember, is it true that every dragon is an expert on something?" she asks, changing the subject.

"Yes, my dear. Magical tapestries are mine. Just like we're born knowing our name, every dragon comes into the world knowing the subject we'll devote our lives to."

"What about Caldera?" Sarah asks. "What's hers?"

"Caldera loves ancient drums. Unfortunately, she wasn't born knowing how to play them." Dr. Ember laughs, and tiny sparks float into the air.

Just as I'm about to ask my next question, Dr. Threadgill walks in with our class following behind. Everybody stares at Dr. Ember. I notice Mrs. Frisner is wearing her dragon socks. They're bright yellow with the blue Puffy Pals marshmallow dragon all over them. She got them when she mailed in twenty empty bags of Puffy Pals.

"Ernestine," Dr. Threadgill says to Dr. Ember, "we're going to my office to take a quick peek at the baby, if you don't mind. They got to see her before she hatched."

"And some of us right after," Ava says under her breath.

"Of course, my dears!" Dr. Ember says. "She's probably still sleeping, so be extra quiet please."

Mouths hang open when our class walks past Dr. Ember, but she pretends not to notice. When you weigh ten tons and are twenty feet tall, you probably get stared at a lot.

"Why don't we all go take a peek," Dr. Ember says to us, and she follows behind our class. A dragon playpen sits next to Dr. Threadgill's desk with a mobile hanging above it. "Rock-a-bye Baby" plays as different gems and gold pieces go around and around in a circle.

There's only one problem. There's no baby dragon.

"Caldera!" Dr. Ember gasps and angry puffs of smoke pour out of her nostrils.

"Help! Security!" Dr. Threadgill yells. "Mr. Hobb will know what to do!" she says, running out of her office and toward the exhibit.

"C'mon," Lily says to me, Sarah, Ava, and Najeeb. "We've got to help my mom!" But when we reach the exhibit floor, there's no Mr. Hobb, either.

"I have a funny feeling . . . ," Ava says. "When we were doing research, I read that where there's a dragon, a goblin's not far away. And Mr. Hobb was one creepy dude. You don't think . . . ?"

"Remember that article I found?" I ask. "Baby dragons are worth more than gold, because they'll lead you straight to their mother's treasure hoard."

"And he smelled weird," Tiger says.

"Tiger has the best sense of smell," Najeeb says. "He's better than a bloodhound. Can you tell which way he went, buddy?"

Dr. Threadgill is talking into a red security phone that's bolted to the wall.

Tiger sticks his nose in the air and sniffs, then points. "That way!"

Lily takes off running, and we all follow her out of the tapestry exhibit. "Hey!" she shouts. "Drop the dragon!" A figure with a sack thrown over its shoulder disappears into the suits of armor.

"How do we find him?" Sarah asks.

We run down the exhibit hall. "Look for the knight who's breathing!" I yell.

CHAPTER 9
A THIEF IN THE KNIGHT

LILY STOPS. "HE'S HERE SOMEWHERE. THERE'S NO other exit. You go that way," she whispers to me, Ava, and Sarah, pointing down an aisle of armor. "And we'll go this way," she says, leading Najeeb and Tiger down another. We step as quietly as we can, inspecting every display we pass.

"I still think this place is spooky," Ava says to herself, peering into a glass case with a knight holding a shield.

"That one's blinking!" Najeeb shouts.

One of the suits of armor jumps off the exhibit stand, shedding pieces as he goes, the sack thrown over his shoulder. We run out of the Hall of Armor, and Mr. Hobb disappears into the mouth of the tunnel leading to the Museum of Natural History.

"This way!" Lily yells.

The tunnel is dim and looks like a mine shaft; it spits us out in the Hall of Gems. Jewels in all colors of the rainbow are inside thick, clear display cases, and there are signs all over. DO NOT TOUCH! EXHIBIT GUARDED AT ALL TIMES. YOU ARE ON CAMERA!

"That's welcoming," Ava says.

"What do we do now?" Sarah asks, looking around.

A puff of baby dragon smoke rises from behind the display case holding the world's second largest diamond.

"We follow him!" Najeeb says.

Caldera pokes her little head out of the sack as Mr. Hobb runs. Puffs of smoke and sparks rise in the air as she grabs at every jewel they pass.

We follow them into the Hall of Ancient Egypt and an exhibit called "Where's Your Mummy?"

I read the sign above the entrance out loud. "What's it like inside a pyramid?"

"It's dark. That's what it's like," Ava says as we run through a maze of twists and turns.

We exit into the museum's Great Hall and come face-to-foot with a brachiosaurus skeleton.

"There he goes!" Najeeb shouts as Mr. Hobb runs

into Dinosaur World.

When I was a little kid, Dinosaur World was my favorite place in the museum. You enter through Jurassic Forest, followed by Cretaceous Land, and end in the Triassic Timeline gallery.

At a distance, Mr. Hobb runs into Cretaceous Land with Caldera. We're about to take off after him when the floor shakes. It feels like an earthquake, and a shadow the size of skyscraper fills the entrance of Jurassic Forest. We look up.

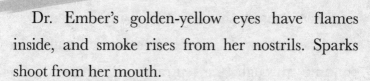

Dr. Ember's golden-yellow eyes have flames inside, and smoke rises from her nostrils. Sparks shoot from her mouth.

Some dragons are nerdy. Some dragons are shy. But this dragon is ANGRY.

CHAPTER 10
MUM'S THE WORD

DR. EMBER LOWERS HER ENORMOUS HEAD. HER eye is the size of a basketball, and it widens when she looks at me, "Where is my baby?"

"That way," I say, pointing in the direction Mr. Hobb ran with Caldera.

"Thank you, Julian," she whispers, raising her head.

Dr. Ember runs across the exhibit hall. All the dinosaur skeletons rattle and some of the floor tiles crack. We follow behind, running past the brachiosaurus and stegosaurus and into Cretaceous Land. Her head almost scrapes the ceiling, and she slams her tail, destroying a fake fern.

"Hey!" Najeeb shouts at her, pointing up at a T. rex skeleton, but it's too late. Dr. Ember is already running through the entrance to the Triassic Timeline and can't hear him.

Mr. Hobb is halfway up the dinosaur, holding the

sack with Caldera in one hand and climbing its rib bones with the other. His foot slips.

"Don't drop the baby!" Najeeb yells, and he stands underneath ready to catch her if she falls. Caldera's little head pokes out of the sack. Her bottom lip trembles, and a big tear runs down her cheek. It splashes on the floor, making a little puddle.

Tiger lifts Najeeb's cap. "I have to help her. Set me down," he says, pointing at the T. rex.

Najeeb shakes his head. "You'll get hurt."

"I'll be fine," Tiger says. He skitters to Najeeb's shoulder and gives him a pat.

"No," Najeeb clenches his jaw. "Your tail. What if you drop it again?"

"Tail shmail," Tiger says. His voice quivers. "I'll grow another one in thirty days. No biggie."

"You can't climb," Najeeb says. "You don't have sticky feet. And you're afraid of heights."

Tiger plants his little paws on Najeeb's cheeks and looks him in the eyes. "I know what it's like to be scared. I can help her."

Najeeb's hand shakes as he sets his best friend on

the T. rex's pinky toe. Tiger looks up, and his eyes get wide.

"Okay. That's a big lizard." He gulps. "A really . . . REALLY big lizard."

Tiger scuttles over the dinosaur's toe and up his ankle. He climbs up the leg but slides back down. He tries again. Same thing. Another tear falls from Caldera's eye. It lands on Tiger's head, knocking him off the T. rex, and he lands on the ground.

Najeeb scoops him up.

"I'm okay!" Tiger says. "It's all good."

Mr. Hobb climbs higher, and Caldera's crying gives her the hiccups. Little puffs of smoke rise in between sobs.

"What's the plan?" Tiger asks, and everybody looks at me.

"I don't know," I say. "I don't go around with rescue plans in my back pocket."

"Pocket!" Najeeb shouts. "That's it!"

He sets Tiger down and rips his windbreaker off. He unzips an inside pocket and pulls out a thin piece of wood with a tiny hole in the middle. It's as long as a pencil, but flat, and there are flames drawn down one side. Next, he pulls out a thin, wooden stick the same length.

"I forgot this was in here. I carved it the other day." Najeeb puts the wooden stick in the tiny hole. It's a propeller. We've built them and had races before to see whose can go highest. Najeeb always wins.

"We don't have time for games," Lily says.

"This is no game!" Najeeb says. "Give me your shoelace!"

"Why?" Lily asks.

"There's no time, just give me your lace!" Najeeb holds out his hand.

Lily rips the lace out of her left sneaker and hands it over. Najeeb ties one end to the bottom of the stick. He looks at Tiger and pauses.

"C'mon," Tiger says, "together we can save her."

Najeeb ties the other end of the shoelace around Tiger's waist and rubs the stick in his hands. He lets go. The propeller lifts higher and higher.

"I'm coming, baby!" Tiger shouts.

Tiger flies past the T. rex's hip bone and first rib, then the second rib, third, and fourth. Finally, he's eye-to-eye with Mr. Hobb, who snarls and kicks. Tiger lands on the T. rex's shoulder and unties the lace around his middle. The propeller falls to the floor and bounces a few times before it stops. He stands on his hind legs and balances on his toes, then he leaps onto the sack, holding Caldera.

Dr. Ember fills the entrance to Cretaceous Land, throws her head back, and roars. A room full of jackhammers wouldn't be this loud. Everything shakes, including me. I plug my ears as fast as I can as flames shoot across the exhibit hall. It feels like we're inside an oven.

Mr. Hobb climbs higher and higher with Tiger and Caldera until they're on top of the dinosaur's skull. Dr. Ember runs toward us. The T. rex trembles, and Mr. Hobb's feet go out from under him. He grabs on to a sharp tooth and dangles in the air, holding on to the sack with his other hand. It slips between his fingers.

"No!" Sarah yells, but Najeeb catches the sack

before it hits the floor. It's so heavy, it knocks him over. The bag opens and Caldera spills out.

A loud CRACK echoes through the hall.

A T. rex rib bone crashes to the ground. Then another. And another. Mr. Hobb crashes to the ground, too, and soon the T. rex's skull follows. It lands with its open jaws facing the floor, pinning Mr. Hobb. Its teeth are like prison bars.

Dr. Ember bends, stroking Caldera's head with her lime-green claw, "My brave girl."

We race over and help Najeeb stand. He looks around, confused. "Where's . . . ?"

Our eyes land on Tiger at the same time. He's sprawled on the marble floor, eyes shut, not moving. Najeeb runs over and scoops him up. "No . . . ," he whispers, and a tear rolls down his cheek and stains his shirt.

Dr. Ember makes her way over with Caldera riding on her back. "Let me help, dear," she says, reaching down and taking Tiger's limp body in her huge purple paw.

Very gently, she rubs Tiger's spotted belly with

the back of her green claw. Nothing happens. She rubs again.

"Come on, little one," she says. "You can do it."

Still, nothing happens.

Najeeb buries his face in his hands. His shoulders shake when I put my arm around him. A tear rolls down Caldera's cheek and splashes on the marble floor. Dr. Ember closes her eyes, and the rest of us bow our heads.

"Hey . . ." A tiny voice breaks the silence. It's so soft I can barely hear it. "What did the green grape say to the purple grape?"

Our heads snap up. We're too stunned to answer.

Tiger opens one eye and looks up at us. "Breathe," Tiger says. "Breathe!" He sits up in Dr. Ember's big paw.

Najeeb laughs as another tear splashes onto his shirt. Dr. Ember lifts her paw, so she and Tiger are eye-to-eye.

"My goodness, we are alike," she says with a smile.

Tiger's eyes widen, and he doesn't move a muscle. "We are?" he squeaks.

"Oh yes. You have the eyes of a dragon. Did you know that?" Dr. Ember asks.

Tiger shakes his head slowly, staring into her golden-yellow eyes. "I do?"

"Yes, my dear. And you fly like a dragon," she goes on.

"No, no, no." Tiger shakes his head. "That was all Najeeb. He made the propeller. I can't fly." His shoulders slump.

"How you did it isn't important," Dr. Ember says. "What matters is that you were brave enough to try. Which leads to the most important thing we have in common."

"What?" Tiger whispers.

"You have a dragon's courage," Dr. Ember says.

Tiger sits taller. "I do? I do!" he says as Dr. Ember bends and places him in Najeeb's cupped hands.

"I've never seen any as brave as the two of you." She gives a sharp-toothy smile and turns, taking Caldera from her back to cradle in one arm.

The dinosaur skeletons rattle as she makes her way back to Mr. Hobb.

"Come on, loves," she looks over her shoulder at us. "Time to get rid of the rubbish."

"Did you hear that?" Tiger asks, riding on Najeeb's shoulder as we head back through the museum. He wiggles his tail. "I'm basically a dragon! Except for the fire-breathing thing or being thirty feet tall."

"I heard, buddy," Najeeb says. "And in my book, you're even better!"

Caldera blows tiny sparks at Mr. Hobb's behind.

"I'm glad this has a happy ending," Sarah whispers.

"Well, that depends on who you ask," I say. "I doubt Mr. Hobb's end is very happy right now."

"Good one, Julian!" Tiger says. "Delivered like a true comedian!"

"Thanks!" I say. "That means a lot coming from such an extraordinary Ordinary!"

CHAPTER 11
UP IN FLAMES!

OUR WHOLE CLASS STANDS OUTSIDE DR. Threadgill's office, and we watch two policemen take Mr. Hobb away.

"Why would someone do something like that?" Sarah asks.

"Dr. Threadgill and I should have seen it coming," Dr. Ember says. "But we were too excited about Caldera and the exhibit to notice. Where there are dragons, goblins are never far behind. Always looking to get ahold of our treasures. It's an age-old battle, I'm afraid."

Dr. Ember looks down at us. The flames are gone from her golden-yellow eyes, and they're soft and kind again. "I'd like to give you a special gift. Something dragons only give to those who are truly worthy. Climb up, loves!"

Dr. Ember lowers her head, and Lily looks at her mom. Dr. Threadgill smiles and nods at us.

"You mean . . . you're going to give us a ride?" I ask.

Sarah smiles, but then her face falls. "We're going to be thousands of feet in the air with no seat belt."

Dr. Ember's scales look as smooth as glass, but I think back to when Caldera hatched and reach out. My hands stick just enough to let me climb, and once I'm on her back it feels like I'm glued in place.

"You can do it, Sarah!" I yell.

Dr. Ember gives a small chuckle. "There's nothing to worry about, dear. It's perfectly safe. How do you think I brought the tapestries over?"

"She's right," Ava says. "DINO conducted a number of scientific studies. The most recent one proved dragon travel is safer than flying on an airplane."

"My goodness!" Dr. Ember says. "You really do know your science. I believe I'm looking at DINO's newest member. And our youngest."

Ava tries to look serious, but she can't hide her smile.

Lily, Ava, Sarah, and I take our seats behind Dr. Ember's head. We look down, but Najeeb and Tiger are still on the ground.

"I saved the best seat in the house for you. May I?" Dr. Ember says, reaching down and holding out her large purple paw for Tiger to hop on.

Tiger looks at his tail and swallows hard before turning back to Dr. Ember. He puts one toe out, like he's testing the water in a swimming pool. He steps with one foot, then two until he's standing on her paw. Dr. Ember lifts him high in the air and sets him on top of her head while Najeeb climbs on board next to Lily.

"Hit it, Emily!" Dr. Ember says. Lily's mom presses a large, red button on the wall, and a thirty-foot-high garage door opens. It's how they move big things in and out of the museum.

Dr. Ember steps outside and gives us fair warning this time, "Cover your ears, dears!"

She lets out a roar, and a stream of flames shoots high into the sky. She unfurls her wings, and in one giant flap we're off the ground, soaring up, up, up.

"The clouds look so magical," Sarah says.

"They are, dear. Some of them, at least," Dr.

Ember says. "Have you never seen cloud seeds? They look just like cotton balls. You plant them on a full moon, water them for twenty-nine days, and—presto! You have clouds."

Ava looks at me. I shrug, "Hey, you learn something new every day, right?"

With no warning, Dr. Ember tosses Caldera into the air. She falls through the layer of clouds and disappears.

Sarah gasps, "Why did you do that? You have to save her!"

"Give her time," Dr. Ember says. "She has to learn."

A few seconds later, Caldera bursts through the clouds, soaring higher than any of us. She's giggling,

"Mama, look at meeeeeee!"

"Leaping lizards!" Tiger yells. "Flying and talking. Way to go, baby!"

Dr. Ember gives a deep, throaty laugh, and we all laugh, too.

The cars and people look like ants below as we circle the museum, and Mrs. Frisner leads our class back toward school. I can see her dragon socks from all the way up here.

Dr. Ember reaches up and pats Tiger. "See? You're flying."

"Like a dragon!" Tiger holds his head high as the wind rushes past.

Dr. Ember coasts lower and lower until we're

almost back on solid ground. Caldera flies in small circles above us as we land.

We slide down Dr. Ember's back. I'm a little wobbly, at first, when my feet hit the ground.

"Time to head back to school," Dr. Threadgill says.

"Can't we stay, Mom?" Lily asks.

Dr. Threadgill shakes her head. "Mrs. Frisner would miss you."

"I'm not so sure about that," Ava says under her breath.

"Sarah," Dr. Ember says. "Would you like to come back to the museum tomorrow for a personal tour of the tapestries? I'd love to share them with such a talented artist."

Sarah smiles so big the corners of her eyes wrinkle. "Yes! Thank you!" She looks at us. "Can I bring my friends? Can we record you for our podcast?"

Dr. Ember nods, and Caldera scampers over. She plants a tiny kiss on Tiger's nose.

"I didn't know leopard geckos could blush," I say.

"Hey, you learn something new every day," Ava nudges me.

We wave goodbye, and head back to school. Frisner's Prisoner's once again.

"That was totally worth missing science," Najeeb says as we walk.

"I wouldn't go that far," Ava says. "Well, okay. Maybe this once."

"Dragons are terrific," Tiger says. "They're courageous. They fly. And they have great eyes. Don't you think dragons have great eyes?"

"I do, buddy," Najeeb says. He reaches up and gives Tiger a pat.

"Dragons are pretty nice, actually," Sarah says.

"Whoa, whoa, whoa," Ava stops. "Dr. Ember and Caldera are pretty nice. But they're not all dragons."

"Maybe we'll meet another one some time, and we can compare," I say.

Sarah stops and points. "Hey, what's that?"

A pinkish-purplish stream of light shoots straight into the sky. It's coming from our school building. Tiger goes back under Najeeb's cap and peeks out.

"Ugh," Ava says, "fairies again."

"Or pixies," Najeeb offers.

"Maybe gremlins," Sarah adds.

"Well, it's too late to turn back now," I say. "Let's go investigate!"